Native Americans
The First Peoples of New York

Kate Schimel and Lynn George

Rosen Classroom

New York

Published in 2012 by The Rosen Publishing Group, Inc.
29 East 21st Street, New York, NY 10010

Copyright © 2012 by The Rosen Publishing Group, Inc.

All rights reserved. No part of this book may be reproduced in any form without permission in writing from the publisher, except by a reviewer.

Book Design: Chris Brand

Photo Credits: Cover David David Gallery/SuperStock/Getty Images; p. 5 © James Randklev/Corbis; p. 7 © Thomas Gilcrease Institute of American History and Art, Tulsa, Oklahoma; p. 9 MPI/Archive Photos/Getty Images; p. 9 © Nathan Benn/Corbis; p. 10 © Philadelphia Museum of Art/Corbis; p. 11 © National Museum of the American Indian, Smithsonian Institution; p. 13 by Jessica Livingston; p. 15 (inset) © The Corcoran Gallery of Art/Corbis; p. 15 (inset) © Joseph Sohm, ChromoSohm Inc./Corbis; p. 17 Nativestock.com/Marilyn Angel Wynn/Collection Mix: Subjects/Getty Images; p. 17 (inset) courtesy of Paul Baxendale; p. 19 © Bettman/Corbis; p. 20 © Corbis; p. 21 © Collection of the New-York Historical Society.

Library of Congress Cataloging-in-Publication Data

Schimel, Kate.
Native Americans: the first peoples of New York / by Kate Schimel and Lynn George. — 1st ed.
    p. cm. — (Spotlight on New York)
Includes index.
ISBN: 978-1-4488-5739-5 (lib. bdg.)
ISBN: 978-1-4488-5751-7 (pbk.)
6-pack ISBN: 978-1-4488-5752-4
1. Indians of North America—New York (State)—History—Juvenile literature.
2. Indians of North America—New York (State)—Social life and customs—Juvenile literature. I. George, Lynn. II. Title.
E78.N7S35 2012
974.7004'97—dc22

2011006915

Manufactured in the United States of America

Cover Image: This detail of an 1838 painting shows the Lenape tribe of Native Americans watching Henry Hudson's ships arriving.

CPSIA Compliance Information: Batch #WS11RC: For Further Information contact Rosen Publishing, New York, New York at 1-800-237-9932

Contents

The First Peoples of New York 4
The Algonquian and the Iroquois 6
Families and Clans 8
Making Art 10
Iroquois Creation Story 12
The Iroquois League 14
Friends or Enemies? 16
The Fur Trade 18
Different Ideas 20
Native American Culture Lives On 22
Glossary 23
Index 24
Primary Source List 24
Websites 24

The First Peoples of New York

The first peoples in New York were **nomads**. They traveled from the north about 11,000 years ago and spoke an early form of the Algonquian **language**. They lived in the pine forests that covered the area. They moved around to find food. They **hunted** animals for meat and **gathered** wild plants and vegetables.

The Algonquian people were **descendants** of the early nomads. They learned to grow their own **crops** of corn, beans, and squash so they didn't have to move in search of food. Around 700 B.C., they started to build permanent homes in the Hudson River valley and on Long Island.

The Iroquois arrived around the year 1300, after the Algonquian had been there for a very long time. The two groups fought over land and food. They each tried to win **honor** by defeating the other in battle.

> The Algonquian groups, or nations, included the Lenape, Montauk, Mahican, and Adirondack. After moving into New York, the Iroquois separated into many nations, including the Onondaga, Seneca, Cayuga, Oneida, and Mohawk. This photograph shows the Ausable River which runs through New York from the Adirondack Mountains to Lake Champlain.

5

The Algonquian and the Iroquois

The **society** of early Algonquian and Iroquois **tribes** is known as the Woodlands Society. The Algonquian and Iroquois lived beside rivers and lakes, which provided fresh water and fish. They traveled the rivers and lakes in **canoes** made from birch bark.

Woodlands people grew corn, beans, and squash. Once the corn was planted and growing, they planted beans and squash in the same plot. The cornstalks supported the bean and squash plants as they grew.

Woodlands people used stone tools for many tasks. They used stones to clean animal **hides** that would be made into clothing. Men made sharp stone points for their hunting spears. Women used heavy rocks to grind corn that they grew and nuts and berries that they gathered from the forests.

Around 1675, a French explorer named Louis Nicolas drew a picture of Iroquois men fishing from a birch-bark canoe. Nicolas showed how the Iroquois used a net, spear, and other tools to catch fish. He labeled the Iroquois as "sauvages," or "wild people," because he did not know much about their way of life.

La pesche des Sauuages p. 15

passinassiouek Je decris cette pesche ailleur qui est une des
choses tres merueilleuses touchand La f. 19 Pesche
f. 19

Kouabagan

Atikamek

Batchkoupin

eskan

Instrumens pour la pesche

Families and Clans

The Iroquois called themselves the Haudenosaunee *(hoh-dee-noh-SHOW-nee)*, or the "People of the **Longhouse**." A longhouse had a frame made from trees that was covered with birch bark. Several **generations** of a family often lived together in each longhouse. Groups of families made up a **clan**. Each tribe had several clans.

In the Iroquois tribe, women raised the crops and owned the land. The oldest women in each clan were called the Clan Mothers. They chose each village's **leader**.

Men hunted, fished, and fought. They also handled the tribe's business. Young men trained for battle by playing **lacrosse**. The game taught them bravery and honor. It was even used to settle arguments between villages.

> The young Iroquois men played lacrosse, much like the Plains Indians are doing in this painting. Lacrosse is a battle-like game involving sticks. The smaller picture shows an Iroquois longhouse and a man wearing traditional Iroquois clothing.

longhouse

Making Art

The Algonquian and Iroquois made very different kinds of art. The Algonquian made beautiful woven baskets for carrying and storing things. Early Algonquian baskets were made of bark, buffalo hair, and leaves. They learned how to make baskets from thin strips of wood. They painted shapes on the baskets.

The Iroquois were famous for the way they decorated clothing and moccasins. They used porcupine quills, which they plucked, dyed, and flattened. It took great skill and a lot of time, a month or even longer, to create just one piece of clothing. Because of this, people valued clothing decorated with quills very highly.

Quills and beads decorate this pair of moccasins from around 1900. The above portrait of Oneida chief Shikellamy, who died in 1748, shows quill decoration on his clothing.

11

Iroquois Creation Story

Native Americans told myths to explain their world and to share knowledge. The most important Iroquois myth, called a **creation story**, was about how the world was made. It says that long ago the whole world was covered in water. Sky People lived in the heavens above. They were led by the Sky Chief.

One day, his wife, Sky Woman, fell through a hole in the sky. As she fell, animals on Earth gathered mud from the bottom of the ocean. They piled it on the back of a turtle to make a world for her. This became the human world.

The Iroquois believed that the world was filled with powerful spirits. Evil spirits could disrupt the world and make problems. Good spirits were able to make the world right again. The Iroquois had special ceremonies that called on the good spirits for help and support.

As Sky Woman fell, swans caught her and slowed her fall. The turtle waited in the vast ocean below for the muskrat to bring mud up from the bottom of the ocean.

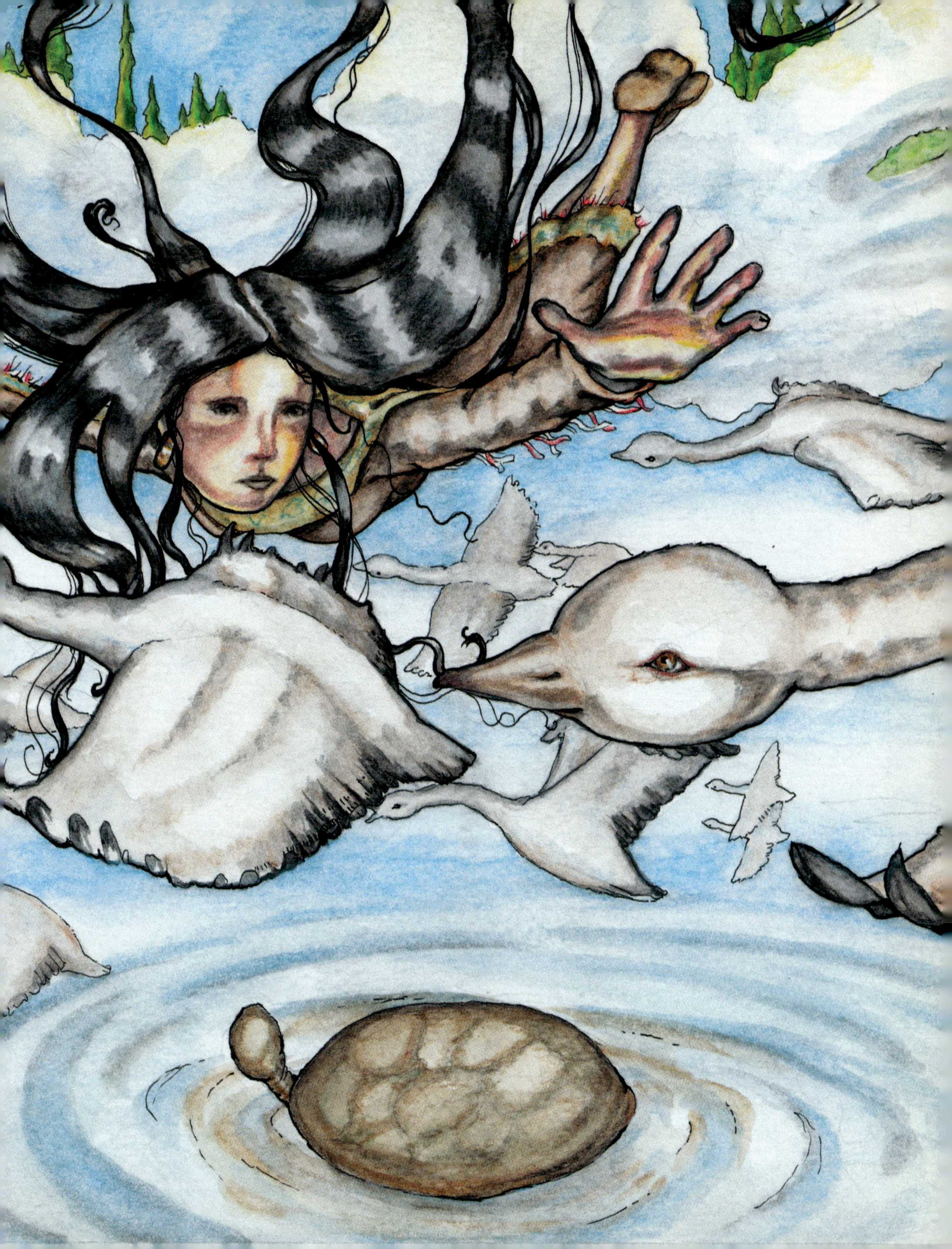

The Iroquois League

For a long time, the Iroquois tribes, or **nations**, each governed themselves. Sometimes they fought each other. More than 500 years ago, a man known as Peacemaker created the **Iroquois League** to stop the fighting. A man named Hayenwatha *(hy-uh-WAH-thuh)* and a woman named Jingosaseh *(gee-GON-sah-say)* helped him. Five nations joined: the Cayuga, Mohawk, Oneida, Onondaga, and Seneca.

Peacemaker wrote a **constitution** for the league. It said that leaders from all five nations would talk about issues that involved all of them. Each nation had the right to make decisions on matters regarding its own people.

The constitution divided the leaders into three groups. The Mohawk and Seneca leaders were one group. The Cayuga and Oneida leaders were another. Both groups agreed on an action. Then the Onondaga made the final choice. The Onondaga were known as the "Fire-Keepers," since they maintained the group's meeting place.

> The early leaders of the United States borrowed many ideas from the Iroquois League when they wrote the U.S. Constitution.

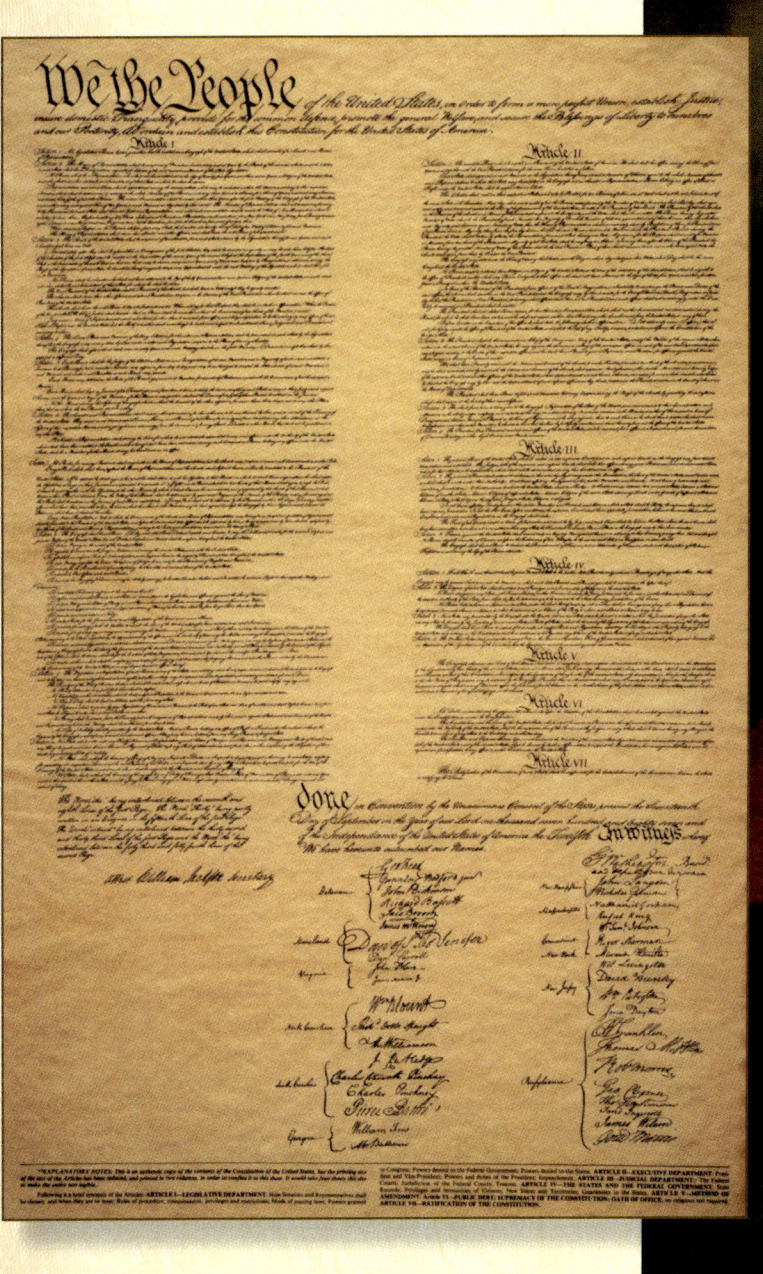

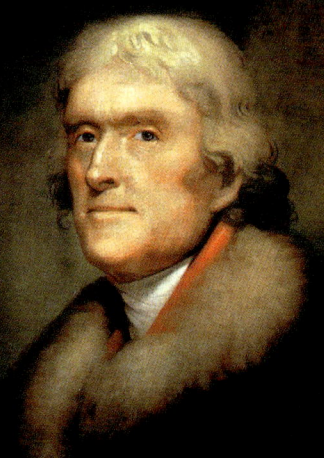

Thomas Jefferson

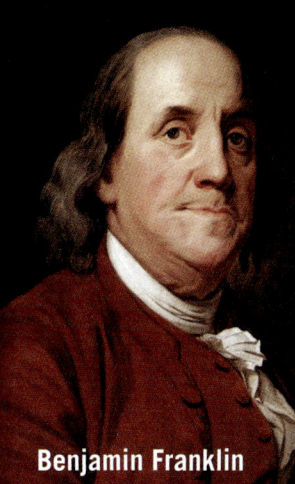

Benjamin Franklin

James Madison

Friends or Enemies?

Since the Algonquian and the Iroquois lived near each other, they often traded. The Iroquois traded food and tools for Algonquian beads. The Algonquian made white and purple beads from seashells. These were called **wampum** beads, and both groups used them to make belts. These belts were records of their history, like a book or a painting.

The two neighbors often fought over land or **goods**. Around 1570, the Iroquois started a war to drive the Algonquian from the area. The war, one of many fought over the years, lasted about 50 years. By the end, the Iroquois **controlled** most of New York.

The Algonquian used sea shells, such as the ones in the smaller photo, to make white and purple beads. They arranged these beads in patterns and weaved them into wampum belts. These belts could be arranged in patterns to record events and treaties.

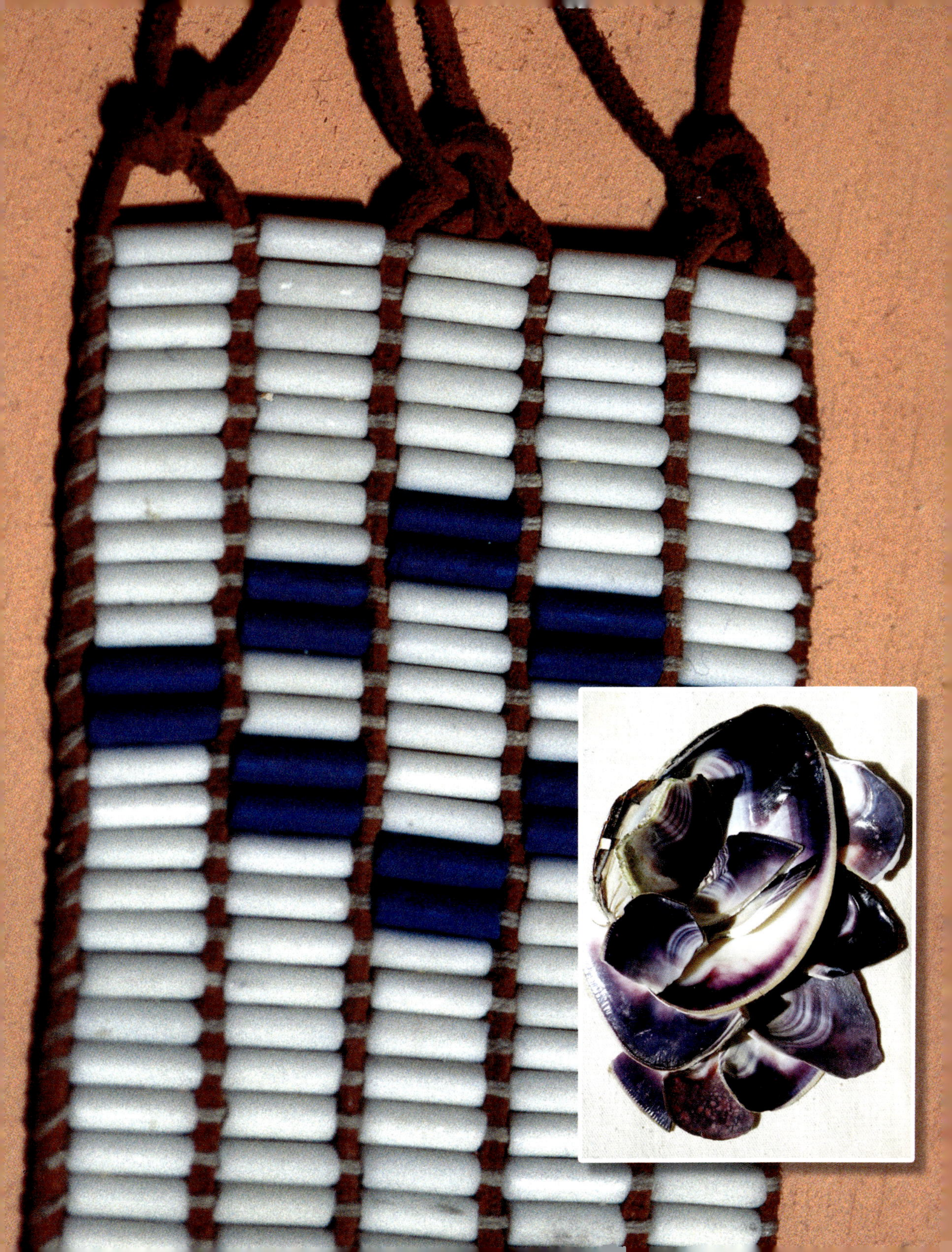

The Fur Trade

European **explorers** arrived on the northern Atlantic coast of North America around the year 1524. One of the first explorers, Giovanni da Verrazzano, met the Lenape Native Americans. He admired their culture and wrote about them in his reports on the land. Soon more European explorers started coming to the area. They wanted to trade with the Native Americans. By the early 1600s, Dutch settlers started arriving in North America wanting to trade for furs. They traded guns, knives, and other tools for beaver furs.

The Algonquian and the Iroquois fought each other for control of the fur trade. These terrible battles were called the Beaver Wars and lasted for 70 years. The guns the Native Americans had gotten from the Europeans caused many more deaths than there had been in past wars.

Europeans also brought with them illnesses that had never before existed in the New World. Tens of thousands of Native Americans died from these new illnesses.

The Algonquian first met Europeans when John Cabot, exploring for England, reached Canada in 1497. By the time French explorer Jacques Cartier arrived in 1534, the Algonquian welcomed him. This picture shows Native Americans greeting Henry Hudson, who came to explore for the Dutch in 1609.

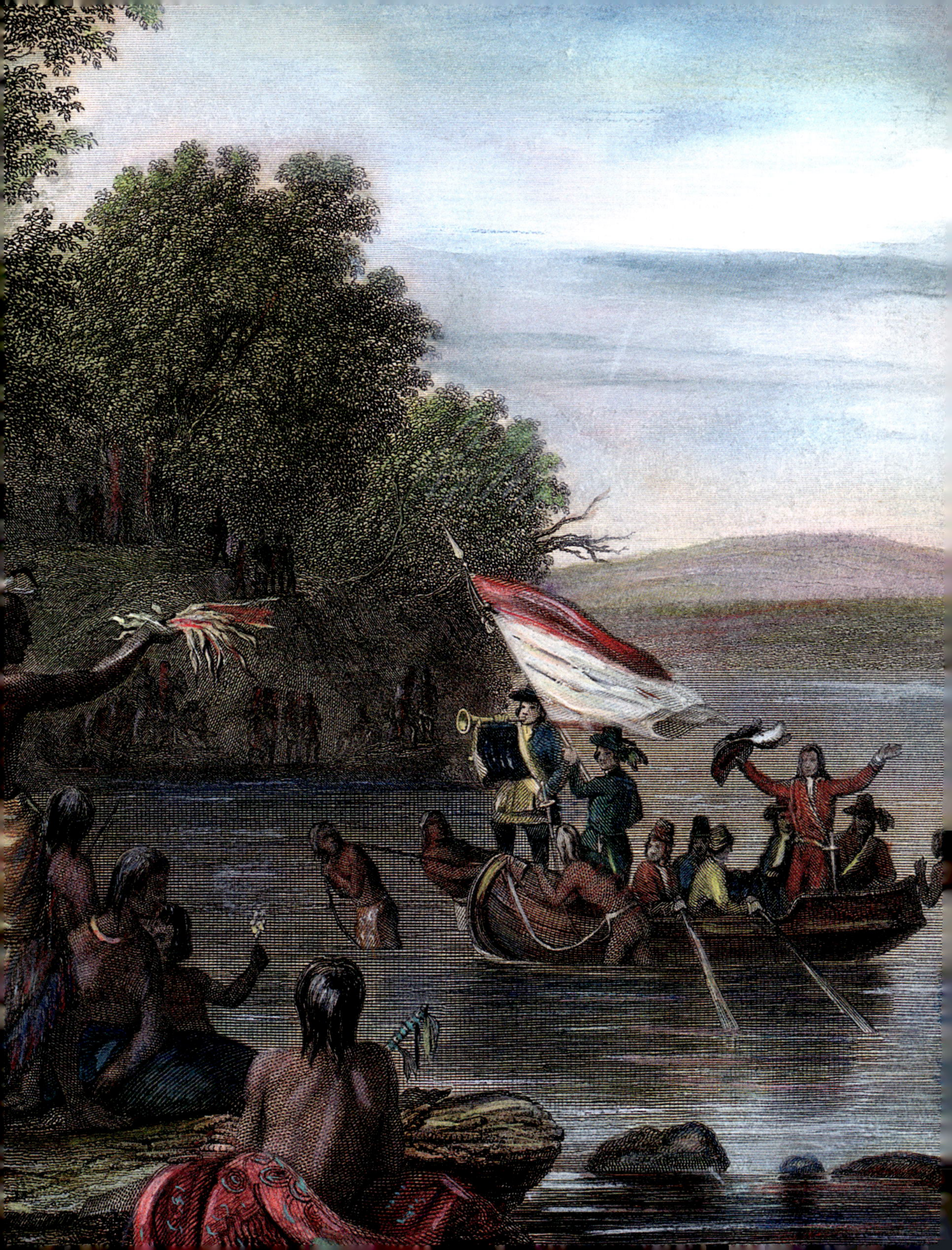

Different Ideas

European ideas were very different from Native American ideas. Settlers tried to get the tribes near them to become more like them. Many Native Americans became Christian. Joseph Brant, a Mohawk leader, and Handsome Lake, a Seneca leader, combined Christian ideas with their ancient beliefs and worked to get other Native Americans to do the same.

Colonists thought that people owned the land. For Native Americans, land was for everyone to use as long as they treated it with respect. Native Americans thought they would be allowed to use the land after the colonists bought it from them. The colonists thought the Native Americans were not using the land since they had not farmed most of it. The two groups did not understand each other.

Joseph Brant

This is part of a paper that records the sale of some Native American lands in New York to the Dutch in 1686. Native Americans "signed" their names with picture characters, seen here near the middle of the page.

Wy ondergeschreven Gekameeck en Mattehaes
Mahikanders, bekennen [illegible] verklaren dat
alsoo wy aen Robbert Sanders een merckelycke
somma van betalinge schuldigh syn aen hem *
verbonden, alle onse gerechtigheid en eygendom die
wy hebben [illegible] Schaahkoock, welcke so langhe sal
staen gerepten tot dat wy hem hebben ten volle [illegible]
voldaen, [illegible] wanneer dese stadt Albany het [illegible]
Lant sal comen te koopen, so sal dito Robbert
Sanders het gerechte waerde vant Lant, so [illegible]
dan van [illegible] wert gedaen, voldaen worden
In kennisse der waerheyt hebben dat met onse
handen onderteeckent, [illegible] 11 [illegible] in Albany 16[illegible]

* als by syn boeck kan blyken

Robert Sanders [illegible]

Dit is het 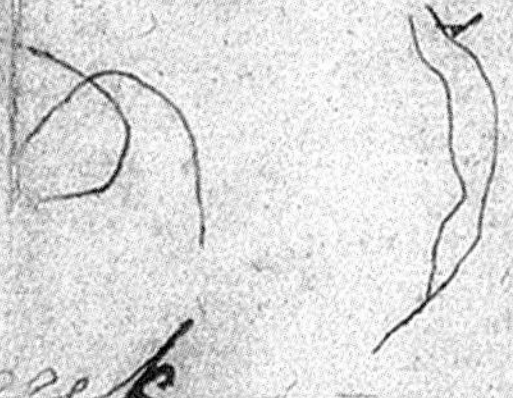 merck van Mattehamout

Geka 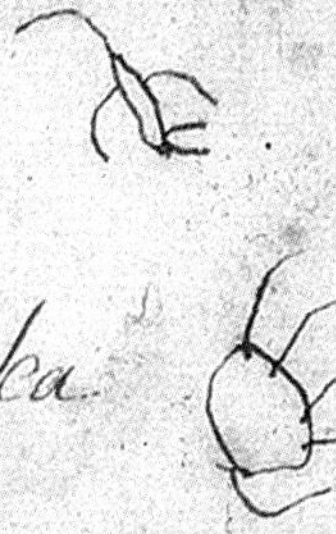 meeck.

Dit is het merck 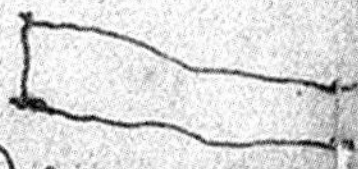 van Mattehaes

Als Tolck van dese bewerent [illegible]

Abram Schuyler

Abraham [illegible]

My present J. Becker Notaris Publiq

Recorded in ye Book of Transports & mortgages
held for ye Citty and County of albany No 2
[illegible] 1691 the 11th day of may 1691

Native American Culture Lives On

The names of many places in New York help us learn about the state's Native American past. Seneca Lake and Oneida Lake are named for the nearby Iroquois nations. The name Manhattan comes from the Lenape word Mannahatta, which means "land of many hills."

There are other parts of Native American **culture** that still exist today. Lacrosse has become a popular sport. It is one of the fastest growing sports in America. The important role women played in Iroquois society inspired American women in the 1800s to seek more rights for themselves, such as the right to **vote**. Perhaps the most important reminder is the U.S. Constitution. It might have been very different without the example of the Iroquois constitution.

Glossary

canoes: Light, narrow boats that are moved by paddling.

clan: Group of families.

constitution: A written set of rules by which a state or nation is governed.

controlled: Held authority over.

creation story: An explanation for how life began.

crops: Plants that are grown and rotated to be used by people.

culture: The beliefs, practices, and arts of a group of people.

descendants: People who are the offspring of people who lived before them.

explorers: People who travel to a new place to learn new things.

gathered: To have found and collected food in nature.

generations: A group of kin born and living at about the same time.

goods: Items that can be produced, bought, or sold.

hides: The skins of animals.

honor: Regard with great respect.

hunted: To have killed animals for food.

Iroquois League: A group of Native American peoples made up of the Mohawk, Oneida, Onondaga, Cayuga, and Seneca tribes.

lacrosse: A game invented by Native Americans.

language: The speech of a group of people used to communicate.

leader: A person who is in charge of or in command of others.

longhouse: A large, long house that is home to several connected families.

nations: Groups of people who share a common history, culture, and often, language.

nomads: People who move from place to place with the seasons.

society: A group of people who share a common bond.

tribes: Groups of people who have the same ancient kin and follow the same way of life, generally in Native American cultures.

vote: The act of choosing a leader or law.

wampum: Small, tube-shaped bead made of shell.

Index

A
Algonquian, 4, 6, 10, 16, 18, 22

B
Beaver Wars, 18
Brant, Joseph, 20

C
Cayuga, 14

H
Handsome Lake, 20
Haudenosaunee, 8
Hayenwatha, 14

I
Iroquois, 4, 6, 8, 10, 12, 14, 16, 18, 22
Iroquois League, 14

J
Jingosaseh, 14

L
lacrosse, 8, 22
Long Island, 4

M
Mohawk, 14, 20

O
Oneida, 14
Onondaga, 14

P
Peacemaker, 14

S
Seneca, 14, 20
Sky Chief, 12
Sky People, 12
Sky Woman, 12

W
wampum beads, 16
Woodlands Society, 6

Primary Source List

Cover. *Landing of Henry Hudson.* Oil painting by Robert Walker Weir, 1838. Currently held at a gallery in Philadelphia, Pennsylvania.

Page 7. *La pesche des sauvages* (Native Americans fishing). Drawing by Louis Nicolas in his manuscript, *Codex Canadiensis*, around 1675, in the Gilcrease Museum, Tulsa, Oklahoma.

Page 9. *Choctaw Ball Game.* Painting by George Carlin, around 1835.

Page 10. *Portrait of Chief Shikellamy, Oneida.* Painting by an unknown artist, around 1725–1748, in the Philadelphia Museum of Art.

Page 11. Quilled and beaded Seneca moccasins, around 1900, in the Smithsonian Institution, Washington, D.C.

Page 15. U.S. Constitution, 1787; in the National Archives Building, Washington, D.C. Portrait of Thomas Jefferson, by Gilbert Stuart, around 1805–1807; at Bowdoin College, Brunswick, Maine. Portrait of Benjamin Franklin, by Joseph Wright, 1782; in the Corcoran Gallery of Art, Washington, D.C. Portrait of James Madison, by Gilbert Stuart, around 1809–1817; in the National Gallery of Art, Washington, D.C.

Page 20. *Portrait of Joseph Brant.* Engraving and etching by an unknown artist.

Page 21. Deed conveying land from Native Americans to Dutch colonists, 1686, in the New-York Historical Society.

Websites

Due to the changing nature of Internet links, The Rosen Publishing Group, Inc. has developed an online list of websites related to the subjects of this book. This site is updated regularly. Please use this link to access the list: **http://www.rcbmlinks.com/nysh/nany**